DOMINOES

Football Forever
Andrea Sarto

Founder Editors: Bill Bowler and Sue Parminter

Illustrated by Kanako Damerum and Yuzuru Takasaki

Andrea Sarto was born in the UK, but has lived and worked in several different countries as an English-language teacher, trainer, and editor. As a child, Andrea's favourite football team was Wolverhampton Wanderers, who were once very good. As a teenager, Andrea liked the purple kit of Fiorentina, but now supports Barcelona like everybody else. The best features of Andrea's own game are ball control and a strong, left-foot cross.

OXFORD
UNIVERSITY PRESS

OXFORD
UNIVERSITY PRESS

Great Clarendon Street, Oxford, OX2 6DP, United Kingdom

Oxford University Press is a department of the University of Oxford.
It furthers the University's objective of excellence in research, scholarship,
and education by publishing worldwide. Oxford is a registered trade
mark of Oxford University Press in the UK and in certain other countries

© Oxford University Press 2016

The moral rights of the author have been asserted

First published in Dominoes 2016

2020 2019 2018 2017 2016

10 9 8 7 6 5 4 3 2 1

No unauthorized photocopying

ISBN: 978 0 19 460913 5   Book
ISBN: 978 0 19 462239 4   Book and Audio Pack

Printed in China

This book is printed on paper from certified and well-managed sources

ACKNOWLEDGEMENTS

The publisher would like to thank the following for their permission to reproduce photographs:
Getty Images pp.iv g (Pele/Eric Schweikardt/Sports Illustrated), iv h (Brazil vs. Australia
Women's World Cup 2015/William Volcov/Brazil Photo Press/LatinContent), 6 (fans/Peter
Parks/AFP), 40 (Rivaldo/Christophe Simon/AFP), 41 (ladies soccer/Tom Hauck); Oxford
University Press p.iv i (trophy/Photodisc); Shutterstock p.iv f (Flag of Brazil/Sarunyu_foto).
Illustrations by: Kanako Damerum and Yuzuru Takasaki/Good Illustration Ltd

Contents

BEFORE READING

1 Here are some people from *Football Forever*. Complete the sentences with their names.

Tino

Lenda

Captain America

Coach Zangado

Falcão

a .... teaches and helps the players.

b .... is young. He's playing his first big game.

c .... is big and mean.

d .... is a goalkeeper.

e .... played for Brazil when he was younger.

2 What do you think you are going to read about in *Football Forever*?

a ☐ How people live in Brazil.

b ☐ A famous football player.

c ☐ An important game of football.

d ☐ An expensive Cup.

Chapter One
Half time

'Bad! Very bad!' the **coach** says angrily.

It's the last **game** of the year. We need to **win** to get the **Cup**. 'We' is Stars, my new football **team**, and I'm Albertino, or Tino to my friends.

Our team are losing 2–0 to Stripes. They've got some good players and are playing well, but I know we can play better.

'Bad! Very bad!' the coach says again. They call him 'Zangado' – 'angry' in Portuguese. He looks **around** the changing room. His hair is white, his face is red.

'We must win this game! Do you want to win the Cup or not?'

We want to win, but nobody answers. The players are looking down – all but three of us. The first is my friend, Junior. He's nineteen and comes from my hometown. He's a good player and my best friend. I like him a lot. I remember we played *futsal* when we were children. *Futsal* is football with only five players in the team. It's a fast game!

coach a person who helps and teaches players

game something that you play

win (*past* **won**) to be the best in a game

Cup you get this when you win an important game

team a number of people who play together in a game

around all the way round

The second is Lenda. He's thirty and he comes from São Paulo. He's the **captain** of Stars and a very good player. He played for the Brazilian team when he was younger. I saw him play and I had a picture of him in my bedroom. But he doesn't like me because I'm new... and very young.

The third is me, Tino. I'm only sixteen, but I live football. In the day, I play football; at night, I sleep football. I eat and drink football! The beautiful game! Stars is my first big team and I'm very happy to be here. I know I'm young, but it doesn't matter. I've got two quick feet – I'm not tall, but I'm very fast, and **stronger** than other boys of sixteen. I can play **forever**.

I didn't play in the first half. I waited and watched, but I could do nothing, of course. We went 1–0 down after ten minutes, then 2–0 down five minutes before half time. Ouch!

'OK,' the coach says suddenly. 'I want much more from all of you in the second half. We must play better, so I'm going to make some changes.'

Now all the players look up.

'You and you,' the coach says to two players. 'You worked well, but I'm making two changes.'

'Nakano, are you ready?' he asks a different player.

'Yes, coach,' says Nakano.

'OK. You're on.' Then he looks around. Who's the next player? I feel my hands get hot. Coach Zangado looks past me. Then he looks back. 'Tino, are you ready?'

'Who – me?' I ask.

'Yes – you. You're the only Tino here.'

'Er, yes, coach. I'm ready.'

'OK. You're up front, with Lenda. We need a **goal** early in the second half. Understand?'

'Yes, coach.'

Junior looks at me and gives a big smile. Lenda looks at me, but he doesn't smile. He's thinking, 'Who is this boy? How good is he? Can he help us win?'

I can't answer these questions, but I feel very happy and excited. My shirt is white: number 20 with 'TINO' in big black letters on the back. On the front is a big star. I pull up my right **sock**, then my left. In my left sock there is something for good **luck**: a little star.

sock you wear this on your feet in your shoe

luck when things happen to you that are very good or very bad

3

My mother gave the little star to me when I began to play *futsal*. 'Here, Tino – take this for luck. You're little now, but one day you're going to be a big star, an **amazing** player. I know it. You're going to play for a big team.' I love my mother. She's here today, with my younger brother,

Alex, and my little sister, Talita. My hometown is watching the game on TV, but my father isn't here today.

He doesn't want to come, he says.

'Sshh! Now listen to me,' says the coach. Everybody in the changing room is suddenly very quiet, and we can hear the big clock.

'It isn't finished. OK, we're 2–0 down. Not good. But we've got forty-five minutes. Anything can happen in football, you know that. Stars is a good team; Stripes is an OK team. They've got one good player: their **keeper**. He's a big man and he can stop a lot, but he's only one man. Let's play our game. Move the ball and work for the team. Don't stand and think. Play with your feet, and when you can, **shoot**! This is Brazilian football. It's easy!'

The players are looking at coach Zangado. 'He's right,' says Lenda. 'The game isn't finished. We can do it.'

'But do you want to win?' asks the coach.

'Yes,' some of the players say.

'I can't hear you,' says the coach. 'Do you want to win?' This time all of the players **shout** 'Yes!'

'And can you do it?' asks the coach.

'Yes!' shout the players.

'Come on – we can do it!' the captain shouts. He looks in our eyes. 'OK, let's go!'

amazing very good

keeper (**goalkeeper**) the player in front of the goal who can use his hands to stop the ball

shoot to hit the ball with your foot at the goal

shout to say loudly

We all walk out of the changing room. I've got **butterflies** in me, but I feel good. Butterflies are OK in my first big game! The **fans** shout when we run onto the **pitch**. The noise is amazing. The pitch is very green and it suddenly feels very, very big. I look around. There are thousands and thousands of fans – some in white shirts, some in red shirts. White is our colour; red is the colour of Stripes. They're all watching the game, and watching me. 'Come on, Tino!' I say quietly. I know I can do it!

butterflies an excited feeling before doing something important

fans people who like football a lot

pitch where you play a game of football, usually green

READING CHECK

Are these sentences true or false?

Tick the boxes.   **True**   **False**

a Coach Zangado is angry with the players. ☑   ☐

b It's the first game of the year. ☐   ☐

c Stars are winning 2–0. ☐   ☐

d Stars is Tino's first big team. ☐   ☐

e Tino played in the first half. ☐   ☐

f Coach Zangado changes three players. ☐   ☐

g Tino and Nakano are going to play. ☐   ☐

h Tino thinks his star brings him good luck. ☐   ☐

i The Stars team don't want to win. ☐   ☐

WORD WORK

1 Choose the correct words to complete the sentences.

a I can't find my left *sock* / *luck*!

b The *coach* / *captain* is usually the best player.

c The *fans* / *butterflies* often wear the colours of their team.

d It rained yesterday, so the *pitch* / *game* is really green.

e Did they *win* / *around* the game last night?

f The fans are *shouting* / *shooting* loudly.

g In football, only the *keeper* / *team* can pick up the ball.

h Who's going to win the *goal* / *Cup*?

i We won 5–4. It was an *amazing* / *strong* game!

2 Complete the sentences with the words you did not use in Activity 1.

a A lot of players do things to bring them good ...... luck ....

b She can .... with her right and left foot.

c I always get .... before I go onto the pitch.

d We have a good .... – I've learned a lot.

e You can't get the ball off him – he's too ....

f What time does the .... start?

g Did you score a .... ?

h Look .... before you shoot.

i What's the most famous .... in your country?

GUESS WHAT

Choose from the characters. In the next chapter, who is going to…

a ☐ get a goal? **c** ☐ make an important pass?

b ☐ stop a goal? **d** ☐ give away a free kick?

Tino

Lenda

Zangado

Captain America

Falcão

Chapter Two

Second half

forward a player at the front of a team who usually gets goals

midfielder a player behind the forwards

pass to give the ball to a player when he needs it

tackle to take the ball off a player on the other team

score to get a goal

defender a player at the back of a team who tackles a lot

shot when you hit the ball with your foot at the goal

mean not nice

kick to hit the ball with your foot

My team is playing 3–5–2. I'm up front with Lenda, the captain. He's a **forward** with an amazing right foot.

Our five **midfielders** are all good, but the best one is Bruno. He's from Argentina and can **pass**, **tackle**, and **score** with his right or left foot. I usually shoot with my right foot, but my left is getting stronger.

Our three **defenders** are tall and strong. My friend Junior is a defender – he can tackle really well. He's good with his head and watches the ball carefully, too.

Right now, Stripes have got the ball. They pass it from player to player and then back to the keeper. He's their captain and he comes from the USA: 'Captain America', the fans call him. He's two metres tall, and his big hands and feet can easily stop a **shot**. He changed the colour of his hair for this game – now it's red. Wow! He looks **mean**. He **kicks** the ball eighty metres down the pitch, but our defenders get it and pass it to the midfielders.

I run fast, so no Stripes players are near me.

'I'm free!' I shout, but nobody hears me.

The midfielders pass the ball slowly. Bruno sees me, but doesn't pass it. The ball comes to Lenda, and I make a run through the Stripes defenders.

'Lenda – over here!'

He doesn't pass it. He doesn't want to pass it. I need to kick the ball or my butterflies aren't going to go. Fifteen minutes into the second half and nothing. Right. The ball isn't going to come to me, so... I run back into our half of the pitch. Now my friend Junior's got the ball. I put my hand up and he plays a nice pass to my feet. At last!

Suddenly somebody shouts, 'Man on!'

Oh no! I lose the ball to a Stripes midfielder. I run back and tackle him, but he **falls** over. The **whistle** goes. What? Free kick to Stripes – oh no! The first time I get the ball, and I give Stripes a free kick. The fans shout and I feel bad, but it's going to get worse. The **ref** is walking up to me with a yellow **card** in his hand.

'Bad tackle from behind,' he says.

It's my first game for my new team. Lenda looks at me and he's thinking: 'This boy's no good. He can't help us win. He can only make us lose!'

'Come on, Tino!' shouts Junior, 'It doesn't matter.'

He's right – it's only a free kick. I run and stand next to the defenders. Our keeper's name is **Falcão** and he shouts: 'Four! I want four men in front. Move to the left, more, more!'

fall (*past* **fell**) to go down quickly

whistle a small thing that makes a noise to stop a game

ref (**referee**) the person in football who controls the game; he or she usually wears a black shirt

card the ref can show this for a foul; it is yellow or red

Falcão /fal'kao/

Then the whistle again. A Stripes forward hits the ball with his right foot – a good shot over our heads – but Falcão **saves** it. Yes! I run up to him.

'Good save!'

He smiles with his eyes. 'You give good luck, Tino!'

Five minutes later, I get the ball again, but this time the home fans whistle. Is it because I'm new... or because I gave away a free kick? They want me to go off. Why did I leave my hometown to play for Stars? My father was right. 'Don't go,' he said. 'You're not ready. Stars is a big team and you're very young.'

'But Dad,' I said, 'I watched Stars play when I was six years old. Now I'm sixteen. It's time for me to go.'

'You think you're a man.'

'No, that's not it. I only want to be the best.'

'OK,' he said at last. 'You can go, Tino, but I don't want to watch you play.'

That's why my father isn't here today with my family.

save to stop the ball from going in the goal

Argh! Just then, a Stripes defender tackles me – a really mean tackle. He kicked my leg. Now he's got the ball and I'm sitting on the pitch.

'**Foul**!' I shout.

'No,' says the ref.

No whistle, no foul, and no free kick. And we're 2–0 down. What a game! But I'm not going to stop playing. It's time for me to start. 'Come on, Tino,' I think.

I get up and run after the defender. He passes it to another player, but it's not a strong pass. Can I get there before him? Yes! I've got the ball. I put my foot on it and look up. There are two defenders in front of me, and the keeper. I **dribble** past one defender and then kick the ball between the legs of the other. Now the keeper comes out

foul to tackle a player in the wrong way

dribble to run with the ball at your feet

box one of two small areas in front of the goal on a pitch

high five when you hit a person's hand with your hand because you are happy

to meet me – Captain America, with his mean red hair. How can I get past him? His arms and legs are long, and his hands are very big, too.

'Tino!' Lenda suddenly shouts. He's running into the **box** on my left. I look right, but kick the ball left: a 'no-look pass'. Captain America is big, but he can't move that fast. Lenda hits the ball – a strong shot... he scores! Goal!

Now we're only 2–1 down. The fans shout. All the players in my team run up to Lenda.

'Well done! Good goal!'

Then Lenda comes up to me and gives me a **high five**.

'Nice pass, Tino.' He smiles and I smile back. But then we look at the clock.

READING CHECK

Match the words with who says them.

a Good save!

b I only want to be the best.

c Nice pass, Tino.

d Foul!

e You give good luck, Tino!

f You think you're a man.

g Bad tackle from behind.

h Man on!

1 ☐h A Stars player says this to Tino.
2 ☐ The ref says this to Tino.
3 ☐ Tino says this to the Stars keeper, Falcão.
4 ☐ Falcão says this to Tino.

5 ☐ Tino's father says this to Tino.
6 ☐ Tino says this to his father.
7 ☐ Tino says this to the ref.
8 ☐ Lenda says this to Tino.

WORD WORK

1 Complete the crossword with new words from Chapter 2. The words across (▶) are all players; the words down (▼) are all verbs.

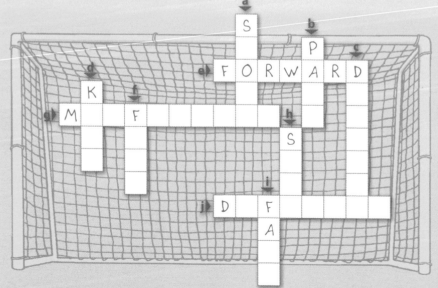

2 Match the words from Activity 1 with the definitions.

1 ☐ to stop the ball from going in the goal

2 ☐ a player at the back of a team who tackles a lot

3 ☐ to run with the ball at your feet

4 ☐ to give the ball to a player when he needs it

5 ☐ a player at the front of the team who usually gets goals

6 ☐ to get a goal

7 ☐ to hit the ball with your foot

8 ☐ a player behind the forwards

9 ☐ to go down quickly

10 ☐ to tackle a player in the wrong way

GUESS WHAT

What is the score going to be at the end of the next chapter? Tick one.

Chapter Three

Three minutes left

Three minutes... there are only three minutes left. Where did all the time go?

My team, Stars, are losing 2–1 to Stripes. The winner of this game gets the Cup. Usually the strongest and best teams win the Cup. I passed to our captain, Lenda, and he scored. But we need one more goal – an **equalizer** – to make the game 2–2.

Most of us are tired, but I didn't play in the first half, so I feel OK. I'm running after the Stripes defenders to get the ball. They take it to the **corner** of the pitch, and watch the clock go down. But I run after them and I don't stop moving. I learned to do this when I played *futsal* as a boy. There are only five players in a *futsal* team, so you run and tackle a lot – all the time.

Two minutes to go. Now I'm running fast and the pitch under my feet is green – a beautiful green. This was different when I was younger, of course. Before we moved to my hometown, I lived in a village. There were no green pitches. Only a dirty, orange pitch under a hot, hot sun. We played football for hours: me and my friends; me and my little brother, Alex. We were all the best players at once. 'And Kaká passes to Robinho, Robinho to **Ronaldinho**, Ronaldinho shoots... he scores!'

I scored a lot of goals on that orange pitch, but today I only need to score one. And I need to score it now. There's one minute left to save the game. Sixty seconds.

The fans are shouting 'Stars! Stars!' Our fans are in white; the Stripes fans are in red. Then one of the Stripes

equalizer the goal that makes the score 1–1, 2–2, etc.

corner where the two sides of the pitch meet; when you kick the ball from here to the goal

Ronaldinho /ʁonaw'dʒĩɲu/

defenders quickly passes the ball to a midfielder. He dribbles the ball up the pitch and passes to a forward. This doesn't look good. The forward goes past a Stars midfielder... and then a defender. Oh no! This Stripes player is good – he gets near the goal and he's going to shoot. I must stop him. I can tackle him, but it's going to be **tough**. Earlier, I gave Stripes a free kick and I got a yellow card! This time, the forward is in the box, so I don't want to give away a **penalty**. Not with only one minute to go and my team 2–1 down!

I run fast and – yes! – I tackle him. No whistle. I've got the ball. Our keeper, Falcão, wants it. 'Tino, pass it to me. I'm going to kick it into their box.' But I don't listen. Something tells me to go, go, go! I dribble past a Stripes player and then do a **one-two** with Junior. I go past another player and then pass to Bruno. All the time I'm running fast. Bruno dribbles it and then passes it back to me. I can see Lenda is running thirty metres away, across the pitch. It's a tough pass, but I hit it first time and the ball goes to his feet.

tough not easy

penalty a shot from in front of the goal because of a foul

one-two when you pass the ball to a player and then that player passes it back to you

halfway line the long white mark between each half of the pitch

cross to kick the ball from the side of the pitch into the box of the other team

jump to move quickly into the air

miss to go to get the ball, but not get it

dive to jump down near the pitch

net this stops the ball when there is a goal

believe to think that something is true

I run across the **halfway line**. Lenda has two defenders in front of him. He goes past one and then looks up. Nobody from Stars is there to help him. Only me. How many seconds are there on the clock?

Lenda takes the ball into the corner. Why? OK, I know! The two defenders go after him. This leaves me free – there's nobody near me. Lenda dribbles around one of the defenders, he **crosses** the ball, and I run quickly into the box. Their keeper, Captain America, **jumps** but **misses** it! Oh no – I'm not going to get there! I **dive** and head the ball. My eyes are open and then they close as I fall on the pitch. Where did the ball go? The shout from the fans tells me where. In the back of the **net**! Gooaall! The equalizer. I did it! We did it! I can't **believe** it. To score in my first game is amazing, but to score the equalizer is *really* amazing!

16

I hear the whistle and the Stars players run up to me.

'Tino – you did it! What a goal! Wow!' Everybody jumps on me.

I can hear the fans: 'Tino! Tino! Tino!'

I can't believe it. We've got a **chance** to win. The game's going to go to **extra time**.

Now the fans are singing: 'Tino! Tino! Tino!'

I get up as Lenda arrives. He's smiling and he puts his hand on my head.

'Tino, the fans know your name now, I think.'

Then he **claps** his hands and the fans clap with him.

chance if something can happen

extra time more time (usually thirty minutes) so one team can win

clap to hit your hands together to show that you like something

READING CHECK

Who does what in Chapter 3? Choose from the people in the box. You can use each answer more than once.

> **1** Tino   **2** the Stars players   **3** Lenda   **4** the Stripes players
> **5** Captain America   **6** the Stars fans

a ☒ They watch the clock go down.
b ☐ He remembers playing football in a village.
c ☐ He makes an important tackle.
d ☐ He does a one-two with Junior.
e ☐ He crosses the ball into the box.
f ☐ He misses the ball.
g ☐ He heads the ball and scores the equalizer.
h ☐ They jump on Tino.
i ☐ They sing: 'Tino! Tino! Tino!'
j ☐ He claps Tino.

WORD WORK

1 Find eleven more new words from Chapter 3 in the wordsearch.

N	A	B	C	H	A	N	C	E	V	J	P	J
H	E	Q	U	A	L	I	Z	E	R	O	A	T
V	L	E	X	T	R	A	T	I	M	E	B	O
Z	V	L	L	V	B	E	L	I	E	V	E	U
Z	T	C	R	O	S	S	C	L	A	P	A	G
P	M	S	Z	J	U	M	P	M	I	S	S	H
F	P	F	X	Q	G	J	N	E	T	G	I	C
P	E	N	A	L	T	Y	G	A	N	D	C	J
R	G	H	A	L	F	W	A	Y	L	I	N	E

2 Use the words from Activity 1 to complete the sentences.

a That was a foul in the box! It must be a ... penalty ... .

b We're 2–1 down with one minute left. We need an .... fast.

c This is my big .... I have to score.

d A good goal kick goes over the ....

e I'm going to .... the ball, so don't .... it!

f We always .... the other team after the game.

g The shot went into the back of the ....

h The second half ended 1–1. There's going to be ....

i Here comes the cross. Get ready to .... !

j I can't .... how .... it is to win the Cup.

GUESS WHAT

What or who is Tino going to think about in the next chapter?

a ☐ Extra time

b ☐ His hometown

c ☐ His family

d ☐ His first team

e ☐ Coach Zangado

f ☐ The Cup

Chapter Four

Full time

We've got a chance. It's 2–2, so there's going to be extra time. Thirty minutes.

Coach Zangado comes onto the pitch and says to everybody, 'Well played! You got the two goals, but now the real game starts. It's going to be tough, but you can do it. I believe in you. The fans believe in you.'

He gives every player a high five. We're all drinking water and some of us are sitting down on the pitch.

'Get up!' Zangado shouts. 'You're tired, I know. But you're very **lucky** too. You're playing football – the game you love. When you were young boys, you wanted to be here in front of thousands of fans. It was your **dream**, wasn't it? Well, today the dream is true, so be strong and do your best. That's all I have to say. Now listen to Lenda.'

We stand around Lenda for the team talk. We put our arms on the **shoulders** of the players next to us. At first, Lenda is quiet. He looks down and then he looks up – into our faces. His eyes meet our eyes.

'Brothers,' he says, 'when I played for the Brazilian team, we won lots of games. It was easy. We had amazing players and they could do everything. They played for the team. Brazil is football; football is Brazil. Here at Stars, it's no different. Look at Tino. This is his first game for us. He's new, but he runs and runs. He gave away a free kick and got a yellow card, but he also made the pass for the first goal and scored the second.'

I feel my friend Junior's hand on my shoulder. He's smiling at me.

lucky when something happens that is good for you

dream something you want to happen

shoulder this is between your neck and your arm

Then Lenda is talking again, 'Think of this as *your* first game for Stars, too. Work, work, work! Play your best football, but be happy. You're doing this for the team, for your friends and family, for the fans. Remember, we do everything with love – with our **hearts**. Now let's get out there and play! Stars! Stars!'

We jump up and down and sing: 'Stars! Stars!' Then we stand on the pitch and wait for the whistle. I look up at all the people. My family is sitting with the Stars fans. In the first half, I couldn't look at them because I wasn't playing. In the second half, I didn't look at them because I was on the pitch and I was working. I can see my mother – she's

waving. My younger brother, Alex, and my little sister, Talita, are jumping and shouting and singing. But who's that next to Talita? It's my father! My father is here – he came to see me. He smiles the biggest smile and waves at me. I see his mouth move, 'I love you, son. I'm here. I'm here to watch you. I'm sorry.'

'I love you, too,' I shout. Then I **point** to the star on the front of my shirt.

He smiles again and claps his hands. For me, this is wonderful. For me, this is everything.

When I was younger, my dream was to play football. I wasn't different from any other boy, I thought. We all wanted to play football, but we weren't all lucky, I know that now. Some of my friends are at school, and some are working. There are two hundred million people in Brazil. They all love football, but not many can play it for money. There's a chance now for me to be a big star, so I must take it.

heart the centre of feeling in someone

wave to move your hand to say 'Hello' or 'Goodbye'

point to show something with your hand

I'm only sixteen – so what? I'm from a strong family. The photo on my phone is of me, my parents, Alex, and Talita – when we were by the sea last month. The weather there was good and we had a really wonderful time. In the morning, we all played **keepy-uppy** – my mother, too! We had lunch, and then in the afternoon we went in the sea. The sun was very warm. By evening, we were tired, so we sang, or listened to stories. I was happy, but I also know that things change. I'm not a boy any more; I'm a young man.

What's going to happen tomorrow? I don't know. But what's happening today – here, around me – I can see that. This is a really big chance. No butterflies anymore! It's my time and I'm ready.

keepy-uppy a game where you kick the ball up lots of times

23

ACTIVITIES

READING CHECK

Correct the mistake in each sentence.

a There's going to be ~~free~~ time. .....*extra*.....

b Coach Zangado tells the players to sit down. ....

c Tino talks to the team. ....

d The Stars players shout: 'Stars! Stars!' ....

e Tino sees his teacher with the Stars fans. ....

f Tino's mother and sister wave. ....

g Tino points to the star on the back of his shirt. ....

h Tino thinks of a family holiday last year. ....

i Tino remembers playing *futsal* with his family. ....

WORD WORK

1 Find five more new words from Chapter 4. There are extra letters. Write the extra letters in order. They make a new word from Chapter 4.

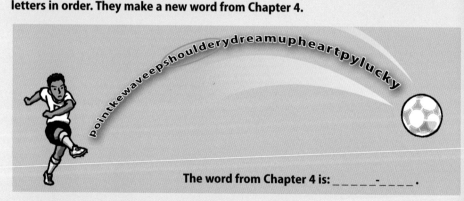

pointkewaveepshoulderydreamupheartpylucky

The word from Chapter 4 is: _ _ _ _ _ - _ _ _ _ .

2 Use the words from Activity 1 to complete the sentences.

a The captain put his hand on my ...*shoulder*... and said, 'Well played'.

b My .... is to play for my country.

c When I run, my .... goes fast.

d Let's have a game of ....!

e ....! We're on television.

f That was a really .... shot. It went in by a centimetre.

g Don't .... at the ref and say bad words.

GUESS WHAT

What happens in the next chapter? Tick the boxes.

a There's a foul and…

1 ☐ Tino gets a red card.

2 ☐ Captain American gets a red card.

3 ☐ the ref doesn't see it.

b Junior scores a goal, but…

1 ☐ the ref says 'No'.

2 ☐ it's in the Stars goal.

3 ☐ has to go off the pitch.

c In the last 30 seconds of the game, …

1 ☐ Tino scores his second goal.

2 ☐ a Stripes player scores.

3 ☐ Falcão makes an important save.

Chapter Five

Extra time

The first half of extra time finishes. The score is 2–2! No goals and not many chances, but now it's the second half and we've got a corner.

Most of the Stars team are in the Stripes box. Only Falcão – our keeper – and one defender aren't there for the corner.

I go to take it. All our players start to move – they want to get free. I put up my hand and then hit the ball with my right foot – a beautiful cross. That's when I see the Stars keeper, Captain America, kick our best player, Lenda. Lenda falls over and Captain America gets the ball easily.

'Penalty!' I shout to the ref.

Lenda gets up and shouts at Captain America: 'Animal!'

But Captain America is two metres tall. He doesn't like it when players shout at him, so he moves his face near to Lenda and looks mean.

'Come on then, old man,' he says.

Lenda isn't afraid of the keeper or his red hair, but then he makes a big **mistake**. In football, you can play tough. You can give 110% and your heart can be hot, but your head must be cold. Lenda kicks Captain America's leg, and the keeper falls over. His hands go to his face. The fans shout noisily and the Stripes players all run to the ref.

It looks bad. Very bad. The ref speaks to his **assistant**, but we can't hear them. Then the ref walks up to Lenda. He's got a card in his hand. What colour? Yellow? Oh no!

mistake when you think or do something wrong

assistant the person who helps the ref

It's red. We've only got ten men and there are five minutes left. What are we going to do without our captain?

Lenda gives the captain's **armband** to Bruno, then he walks off the pitch with his head down. He walks past coach Zangado, but Zangado doesn't speak to him. He's very angry. Lenda kicks over a water bottle and walks off.

'4–4–1!' shouts Zangado to the players on the pitch. 'Strong at the back.' There are five minutes to go. Only five minutes and then – penalties.

But five minutes is a long time with only ten players, and Stripes know it. They can win now, they think, and their players start to move the ball well. One pass, two, three, four – we can't get near it. I'm running fast, but going nowhere. Then a long ball goes to a Stripes forward. He dribbles past one of our defenders and shoots. It isn't a good shot, and it's not going to go into the goal, but then the ball hits Junior on the shoulder. No! Falcão dives, but the ball goes into the net. An **own goal**! I don't believe it. We're 2–3 down. The Stripes team run around the pitch, and their fans are jumping and singing – they're going to win, they think.

armband the captain of the team wears this on his or her arm

own goal when you hit the ball in your team's goal by mistake

I go up to Junior. 'Listen – these things happen. There's time to score an equalizer. We did it before; we can do it again.'

'Why me?' says Junior.

'It's bad luck,' I say, 'and luck can change.'

'With four minutes to go? I don't think so.'

'Let's see.'

The game starts again, but we lose the ball. The Stripes defenders are passing it around slowly. Their fans are clapping. Three minutes left. It's going to take something wonderful. Then we win a **throw-in**. One of our midfielders, Nakano, is going to take it. He can throw the ball twenty-five metres, so I put my hand up. I'm on the halfway line and the ball comes to me. It **bounces** once and I look up. There are five or six Stripes players in front of me and then the keeper, Captain America. He isn't standing on the goal line. He's ten metres in front of it, so I hit the ball first time. Why not?

throw-in to start the game again by passing the ball to a player with your hands

bounce to come down and then go up again

It's an **impossible** shot and it's not going to go in... is it? It bounces and Captain America jumps. His mouth is open in a big 'O'. No! Yes! It goes into the corner of the net. Gooooaaaalll! My second goal. I can't believe it. 3–3! The score is 3–3 with only two minutes to go.

The fans go **crazy**; Junior and the players go crazy; Zangado goes crazy. Impossible! I run round the pitch and shout and jump. This is the most amazing game. But it's not finished.

Stripes start the game again quickly. Every Stars player is back in our half. We make tackle after tackle, but can't get the ball. We're very, very tired. One minute left. Then thirty seconds. We need to get to penalties for a fifty-fifty chance.

Suddenly, one of our defenders falls over – what a mistake! A Stripes forward is through on goal. He shoots. Where is the ball going to go? We can only watch and wait. Falcão dives... and misses it... but the ball hits the **bar**! It hits the bar and bounces back. A Stars defender kicks it over the halfway line and then – at last – the whistle goes.

How lucky can you be? The answer is: *very*.

impossible what cannot be

crazy very excited

bar long metal piece of the goal

READING CHECK

Match the two parts of the sentences.

a	Stars get	**1**	the captain's armband.
b	Captain America kicks	**2**	the bar.
c	Lenda kicks	**3**	an own goal.
d	The ref gives Lenda	**4**	a long shot.
e	Lenda gives Bruno	**5**	a water bottle.
f	Lenda kicks over	**6**	Captain America.
g	Junior scores	**7**	a corner.
h	Tino scores with	**8**	crazy.
i	The Stars players and Zangado go	**9**	a red card.
j	A Stripes forward hits	**10**	Lenda.

WORD WORK

1 The words don't match the pictures. Correct them.

a throw-in	**b** own goal	**c** assistant	**d** mistake
..assistant..	....	....	....

e bar	**f** armband	**g** crazy	**h** bounce
....	....	....	....

2 Complete the sentences with words from Activity 1.

a We lost 3–1. I scored, but it was an ..own goal..!

b The .... is speaking to the ref about the foul.

c In keepy-uppy, you can .... the ball on your head, too.

d Who's wearing the captain's .... today?

e I don't believe it! The ball hit the .... What a ....!

f He's got a very long ....

g Goal! The fans are going ....

GUESS WHAT

How is the story going to finish? Tick one.

a ☐ Tino asks his father for help.

b ☐ Tino takes a penalty in the shoot-out.

c ☐ Captain America saves an important penalty.

d ☐ Stripes win the game and the Cup.

Chapter Six

Penalty shoot-out

All of the players are sitting on the pitch. We're very tired. Coach Zangado walks up to the players one by one.

'Well done! Well played! Amazing game!'

He walks up to me. 'Tino – your second goal was wonderful. Things are going to change for you, I think.'

'Thanks, coach.'

'OK, men,' he shouts. 'Let's look at the names.'

We stand around Zangado and he reads the names of five players for the penalties.

'One: Bruno. Two: Nakano. Three: Victor...'

Is he going to say my name?

'Four: Wesley. Five...'

I listen carefully; we all do. Who's going to take penalty number five, the last one?

'Five: Junior.'

Oh. Not me. But good for Junior! I'm happy for him. I give him a high five. 'You can do it. I know you can.'

We all go and stand on the halfway line, with our arms on the shoulders of the players next to us. I'm standing next to Junior. We wait. Stripes are going to take the first penalty. One of their forwards starts the long walk to the penalty **spot**. The fans are shouting noisily. He puts the ball on the spot and then walks back. Our keeper, Falcão, jumps up and down. He waves his arms. The fans go quiet. The Stripes forward looks **cool**. He waits for the ref's whistle, and then runs and kicks the ball. He scores. That's the first penalty, so it's 1–0. Now it's our **turn**.

Bruno walks up to the spot. He usually takes penalties for the team, so he looks very cool. He shoots. Goal! 1–1!

Now it's Stripes' turn again. This time, Falcão gets his hand to the ball, but it's moving very fast. 2–1.

Nakano walks up to the spot for Stars. He looks at the ball and then at the keeper. Captain America isn't moving; he's looking at Nakano and smiling. He looks very big in the goal. It's a tough question for Nakano – **blast** it or put it in the corner? He blasts it and the net jumps: 2–2.

Then Stripes score again: 3–2.

Then Victor scores the equalizer for Stars: 3–3!

Who's going to miss first – us or them? Not them. They score their fourth penalty. Not us. We score our fourth one, too! 4–4!

This is amazing. The fans can't believe it. Now I'm happy because I'm not taking a penalty!

It's the turn of a Stripes midfielder. He walks to the penalty spot slowly. Has he got butterflies? He puts the ball on the spot and then moves it again. He walks back with his head down. He doesn't want to look at the fans or Falcão. He runs up and hits the ball. Save! Falcão saves it with his legs! For the first time in the game, we've got

spot where you put the ball to take a penalty

cool not excited or angry

turn when it is your time to do something

blast to shoot very hard

a good chance to win. We only need to score the next penalty, and it's Junior's turn.

'Take your time', I say to Junior. 'And remember – don't suddenly change the shot at the last second.'

'OK, I know,' he says and walks up the pitch. We all watch him go. 'This is it,' I think, 'We can win! My friend's going to score this penalty and it's going to get us the Cup.'

When we played *futsal*, Junior took the penalties. He usually put it right in the corner and no keeper could stop it. But what about Captain America?

When Junior arrives at the penalty spot, Captain America walks up and says something to him. Then he puts his hand out for a high five. Junior doesn't give him a high five. Captain America doesn't move, but why doesn't Junior walk away? The ref comes up and points to the goal line.

Captain America smiles and walks back. He opens his arms and stands there. He's looking at Junior, not the ball. His hair is very red. Behind the goal there's a sea of red shirts. The whistle goes. Junior runs up and hits the ball. Oh, no! He blasts it over the bar!

The Stripes players shout 'Yes!' and Captain America stands in front of the Stripes fans. 'Come on!' he shouts, 'Come on!' and the fans go crazy.

I feel really sorry for Junior. First he scored an own goal and now he misses a penalty. He walks back to the team on the halfway line. Is he crying? I put my hand on his shoulder. What do I say? In the end, I say nothing, and Junior can't speak or look at me.

The penalty shoot-out is now **sudden death**. If you miss and the other team scores, that's it. Finished. So who's going to take the next penalty for Stripes? What – the keeper? Captain America? Wow! Nobody can stop him, he thinks.

Captain America walks back to the box. Then he looks at the goal and waits. Our keeper, Falcão, looks little in front of him. Soon, there's the whistle. Captain America runs up and blasts the ball amazingly fast. Falcão doesn't jump – he hasn't got the time. But wait! It hits the **post**... and bounces back. Now the Stars players shout 'Yes!' and go crazy. Captain America can't believe it – he's standing there on the penalty spot.

sudden death when the first team to score one more penalty than the other team wins the game

post one of two tall metal pieces of the goal

Who's going to take the next penalty for Stars? Nobody knows. We look at coach Zangado. He makes a 'T' with his hands. Time out? No. Tino! It's me! He's pointing at me. I've got the chance to win the Cup for Stars in my very first game! And I have a chance to score my third goal! OK, I know that goals in penalty shoot-outs are different. But I'm sixteen years old and for me, that's a **hat-trick**!

The Stars players say 'Good luck, Tino!' I want to look at my family, but there's no time. I start to walk to the penalty spot. It feels far, so I run slowly, with my eyes on the goal. Captain America gets bigger and bigger. I take the ball, put it on the penalty spot and walk away. Then I stop and look down at my socks. I move them up – first my right and then my left. When I do this, I put my hand on the little star in my left sock: the star from my mother.

hat-trick when you score three goals in one game

perfect with nothing wrong

Then I get a crazy idea. I usually hit the ball with my right foot. Captain America is ready for that. But can I shoot with my left? I scored my second goal with my right foot, and my first goal with my head. I need to score this penalty with my left foot to get a **perfect** hat-trick. An amazing, wonderful, crazy idea! Captain America thinks I've got butterflies, but I haven't. I'm cool. I'm the coolest young man in Brazil and I know it's my time.

The fans go quiet. Then the whistle. I move to my right and then start to run. I kick the ball quickly with my left foot. A perfect shot! A perfect hat-trick! Goooooaaaaalllll! I fall on the pitch and smile, then look at my family and wave.

Then my team jumps on me... and the fans and my family and friends and my village and hometown and all of Brazil go *crazy*.

READING CHECK

Put the sentences in the correct order. Number them 1–10.

a ☐ Falcão saves a penalty for Stars.

b ☐ The players sit on the pitch.

c ☐ Captain America's penalty hits the post.

d ☐ Stripes score the first penalty.

e ☐ Tino puts his hand on the little star in his sock.

f ☐ Junior blasts his penalty over the bar.

g ☐ Coach Zangado wants Tino to take a penalty.

h ☐ Coach Zangado reads the names of the players to take penalties.

i ☐ Tino scores the winning penalty with his left foot.

j ☐ Bruno equalizes for Stars (1–1).

WORD WORK

Find words from Chapter 6 in the footballs to complete the dialogues.

a 'Where do I put the ball?' 'At the front of the penalty s p o t.'

b 'Has he got butterflies?' 'No, he looks c _ _ _ to me.'

c 'Now it's my t _ _ _.' 'Oh, I thought it was mine.'

d 'I don't know where to kick it.' 'Just b _ _ _ _ it!'

stop

freeptc

e 'It's a corner.' 'OK – stand near the p _ _ _ .'

f 'That goal was p _ _ _ _ _ _ .' 'Yes, it was an amazing shot.'

tha critk

densud thead

g 'How many goals has he got?' 'Three. It's a h_ _ - _ _ _ _ _ .'

h 'It's 5–5 in the penalty shoot-out.' 'So now it's s_ _ _ _ _ _ _ _ _ _ ?'

GUESS WHAT

What happens after the story? Choose from the ideas or add your own.

a ☐ Tino is captain of Stars.

b ☐ Tino moves to a bigger team in Brazil.

c ☐ Tino breaks his leg in a bad tackle in the next game.

d ☐ Tino moves to a big team in Europe.

e ☐ Tino wins 'Player of the Year' next year in Brazil.

f ☐ Tino plays his first game for the Brazilian team.

g ☐ ....

h ☐ ....

Project A *Game report*

● ○ ○

NEWS

BRAZILIAN HAT-TRICK WINS GAME!

85,000 fans watched the last game of the year: Barcelona against Valencia. The Brazilian forward, Rivaldo, scored after three minutes: an amazing free kick in the corner of the goal. Valencia got the equalizer after twenty-five minutes. At the end of the first half, Rivaldo scored again: a long shot through the defenders' legs. But what a game! Valencia scored the equalizer one minute later: 2–2.

For forty minutes, there were no goals and not many chances. Then, only two minutes before full time, Rivaldo scored his hat-trick. Frank De Boer passed it to him and Rivaldo kicked it over his head with his left foot: 3–2 to Barcelona. A goal in a million from the Brazilian!

1   Put the notes for the report in the correct order. Number them 1–9.

NOTES – Brazilian hat-trick wins game!

- ☐ **a**   at end / first half, Rivaldo / score again: long shot through defenders' legs
- ☐ **b**   Brazilian forward, Rivaldo / score / 3 minutes: amazing free kick / corner / goal
- ☐ **c**   only 2 minutes / full time / Rivaldo score / hat-trick
- ☐ **d**   Valencia get / equalizer / 25 minutes
- ☐ **e**   goal in a million / Brazilian!
- ☐ **f**   what / game! / Valencia / score / equalizer
- ☐ **g**   85,000 fans watch / last game / year: Barcelona vs Valencia
- ☐ **h**   for 40 minutes / there are no goals + not many chances
- ☐ **i**   Frank De Boer / pass it to him + Rivaldo / kick / over / head / left foot: 3–2 to Barcelona

2 Use the notes below to write a report about another amazing game.

NOTES – USA penalty wins World Cup

1 90,000 fans watch / final / Women's World Cup: USA vs China
   90,000 fans watched the final of the
   Women's World Cup: USA vs China.

2 first + second half / there are no goals + not many chances

3 extra time / there are no goals

4 penalty shootout / China miss / third penalty / score /
   4 out of 5

5 USA score / 4 out of 4 / need to score last penalty

6 USA defender, Brandi Chastain / score /
   left foot: 5–4 to USA

7 USA team, fans + all USA / go crazy!

3 Write a short report about the game in *Football Forever*.

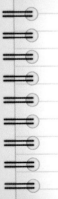

Project B *Post-match interview*

1 **After a game, there is a 'post-match interview' with a good player. Complete the interview with Tino. Put the interviewer's questions in the correct place.**

1 What about the other players?
2 Is your family here today?
3 What did coach Zangado say at half time?
4 How does it feel?
5 What happened in the first half?

Interviewer: So, Tino – what a game!

Tino: Yes, I can't believe we won the Cup.

I: a) ....
....?

T: Amazing! This is the best day of my life. And a hat-trick in my first game for Stars is wonderful.

I: b) ....
....?

T: They're really happy, too. We're all happy because we played as a team.

I: c) ....?

T: I didn't play… It was tough and we started slowly, perhaps. Then suddenly it was half time and we were two goals down.

I: d) ....?

T: He said, 'Stars is a good team' and 'Don't think too much!' He was right. Then after full time, Lenda also talked to us. He said we need to win for the team, for our friends and family, and for the fans.

I: e) ....?

T: Yes, they are. They're all here: my mother, my brother and sister, and – best of all – my father. I'm very happy he saw my first game for Stars. He's going to come to every game from now on!

2 **Complete the interview with Tino's father. Write answers to the interviewer's questions using the notes.**

- yes – surprised; knew Tino was a good player, but not *that* good
- yes – all the time; lived in a village; Tino always played with friends and little brother, Alex
- Ronaldinho for the Brazilian team and Lenda for Stars
- bad luck; Captain America kicked him first, but the ref didn't see it; these things happen in football; happy Stars won the Cup
- all of them were amazing, but perhaps the second one – it was an impossible shot
- didn't know; couldn't believe it; Tino hit it with his left foot, too
- she's very very happy; Tino is her star
- wants to find Tino and tell him he loves him

Interviewer: Well, what about your son?

Tino's father: I know – it's amazing.

I: Are you surprised by how well he played in his first game for Stars?

TF: ....

I: Did he play a lot when he was younger?

TF: ....

I: What players did he like?

TF: ....

I: What do you think about Lenda's red card?

TF: ....

I: Which of Tino's three goals did you like most?

TF: ....

I: Did you know Tino was going to take a penalty in the shoot-out?

TF: ....

I: How does Tino's mother feel?

TF: ....

I: What are you going to do now?

TF: ....

3 Prepare questions for an interview with Captain America or Tino's mother.

4 Imagine you are Captain America or Tino's mother. Prepare answers to the questions in Activity 3.

5 Work in pairs. Roleplay the interview with a partner.

GRAMMAR CHECK

> **Going to future: affirmative, negative and questions**
>
> We make the *going to* future with the verb be + going to + infinitive without *to*. We use the *going to* future for plans, intentions, and predictions.
>
> *I'm going to make some changes.*   *One day you're going to be a big star.*
>
> *The ball isn't going to come to me.*   *What are we going to do without our captain?*

1 Complete the sentences with the affirmative or negative form of *going to*. Who do you think says these things?

Tino

Captain America

Tino's father

a 'I ..`'m not going to watch`.. (not watch) you play in your first game for Stars.'
..`Tino's father`..

b 'I .... (blast) my goal kick over the halfway line!' ....

c 'Oh no! A yellow card. But I .... (stop) playing.' ....

d 'Yes! Stripes .... (win) the Cup!' ....

e 'Is Captain America .... save my penalty?' ....

f 'Come on, Tino! You .... (have) an amazing second half!' ....

2 Write questions about the penalty shoot-out. Match them with the answers.

1 Stripes.	
2 Them, I think.	
3 In the corner of the net.	
4 It's the penalty shootout.	
5 Yes – the first one!	

a what / happen / now? ..`4`..
...... `What's going to happen now?` ....

b who / take / the first penalty? ......
....

c you / take / a penalty? ......
....

d where / you / kick it? ......
....

e who / miss first – us or them? ......
....

GRAMMAR

GRAMMAR CHECK

Imperatives

We use imperatives to give instructions or order someone to do something.

We make the affirmative imperative with the infinitive without *to*.   *Help us!*

We make the negative imperative with don't + the infinitive without *to*.   *Don't go!*

3 **Look at the sentences from coach Zangado's team talk. Some are wrong. Correct them.**

a Don't think too much. ....✔...........

b ~~Think~~ about how tired you are. ....*Don't think*....

c Don't do your best. ....

d Play for the team! ....

e Take your time on the ball. ....

f Don't shoot when you get a chance. ....

g Don't give the ball to the other team. ....

h Remember how lucky you are. ....

i Don't work, don't work, don't work! ....

4 **Put the words from Lenda's team talk in the correct order to make sentences.**

a everything / you / can / give
   Give everything you can...

b watch / don't / clock / the
   ....

c easy / passes / play / the
   ....

d tackles / make / any / crazy / don't
   ....

e good / remember / Stars / team / are / a
   ....

f forget / to / play / don't / with / hearts / your
   ....

GRAMMAR CHECK

Time clauses with *before*, *after*, and *when*

before links a later action with an earlier action.

Before we moved to my hometown, I lived in a village.

after links an earlier action with a later action.

After Captain American missed the ball, Tino scored with his head.

when links two actions close in time.   *The fans shout when the team runs onto the pitch.*

When we write the time clause first, we must use a comma.   *When you can, shoot!*

5 **Complete the sentences with *before* or *after*.**

a The players left the changing room .....*after*..... the team talk finished.

b Look around .... you pass the ball.

c Tino passed the ball .... Lenda shouted to him.

d .... Tino got the ball, he dribbled past three players.

e The ref gave Lenda a red card .... he kicked Captain America.

f .... he kicked the ball, Tino looked at the keeper.

g I'm not going to look at my family .... I take the penalty.

h .... Tino scored the penalty, the team jumped on him.

6 **Complete the sentences about young Tino. Choose from the words in the box.**

> he loved Ronaldinho   ~~he lived in a village~~   he met Junior   he started to play *futsal*
> he watched Stars play   he went to sleep   it was hot   Lenda played for Brazil

a When he was very young, ...*he lived in a village*.....

b He played football on an orange pitch when ....

c When he first played football, ...

d When he was six years old, ...

e There was a picture of Lenda in Tino's bedroom when

....

f His mother gave him a little star when ....

g .... when he played *futsal* in the same team.

h When ...., he dreamed of football.

GRAMMAR CHECK

feel and *look* + adjectives

We use feel + adjective to talk about feelings on the inside.

I feel very happy.

We use look + adjective to talk about feelings or appearance from the outside.

He looks sad today.   *With his red hair, Captain America looks mean.*

We can also use it/non-personal subject + feel + adjective to mean 'give somebody a feeling'.   *The pitch feels really big.*

7 Complete the sentences the with adjectives in the box.

amazing   angry   bad   ~~excited~~   fast   mean   tired

a Tino is going to play his first game. He feels … *excited* … .

b Zangado's face is red. He looks . . . .

c Tino is young and strong. He looks . . . .

d Wow! Captain America looks very . . . .

e Junior missed the penalty. He feels . . . .

f Tino scored the penalty. He feels . . . .

g The Stripes players are sitting on the pitch. They look and feel . . . .

8 Write sentences about Tino's feelings at the start of the second half.

pitch = big   time = slow   head = cold

hands = hot   heart = fast   sun = warm

a . Time feels slow . . . .   **d** . . . .

b . . . .   **e** . . . .

c . . . .   **f** . . . .

GRAMMAR CHECK

Negative structures with *nothing*, *nobody*, and *nowhere*

nothing means 'no thing', or 'zero'.

I've got nothing in my bag.

nobody means 'no person'. We can also use *no one*.

I shout, but nobody hears me.   *No one knows what to do.*

nowhere means 'not in or to a place'.

There's nowhere to go.

nothing, nobody, and nowhere are already negative. We do not use *not* or *n't* with them. We use a singular verb after them.

Nothing matters.   *Nothing doesn't matter.*   *Nothing matter.*

9 Complete the sentences with *nothing*, *nobody*, or *nowhere*.

a In the first half, there's ....ṇọṭhịṇg.... Tino can do to help Stars.

b 'Do you want to win?' asks Zangado, but .... answers.

c At the start of the second half, ... passes to Tino.

d Tino's running fast but going ....

e Lenda walks off, but Zangado says ....

f '................. can stop us winning the Cup,' thinks Captain America.

g Captain American is big; the goal is little. There's .... to kick the ball.

h .... is going to be the same again for Tino.

10 Match the first and second parts of the sentences.

a Nobody scores,   **1** to pass to.

b Nothing   **2** so nobody wins.

c Nobody has   **3** nowhere near the goal.

d Nobody is   **4** got green hair.

e The shot goes   **5** taller than Captain America.

f There was no one   **6** is more important than the Cup.

GRAMMAR CHECK

Comparative adjectives

We use -er to make the comparative form of most short adjectives.

tall   *taller*

When short adjectives finish with consonant + y, we change y to i and use -er.

happy   *happier*

When short adjectives finish with consonant + e, we use -r.

nice   *nicer*

When adjectives finish with short vowel + single consonant, we double the last consonant and use -er.   *big*   *bigger*

With longer adjectives (other 2 syllable adjectives, or adjectives with 3+ syllables), we put *more* before the adjective.   *amazing*   *more amazing*

We use comparative adjective + *than* when comparing two people.

Tino's father is older than his mother.

11 Write comparative sentences about Tino and Junior.

a (young)   Tino … *is younger* … than Junior.

b (lucky)   Tino . . . . than Junior.

c (amazing)   Tino . . . . than Junior.

d (cool)   Tino . . . . than Junior.

e (tall)   Junior . . . . than Tino.

f (old)   Junior . . . . than Tino.

12 Complete the comparative sentences about other people in the story.

a Zangado is o *l d e r t h a n* Tino's father.

b Tino is s _ r _ n g _ _ _ _ _ _ other boys of sixteen.

c Falcão is n _ c _ _ _ _ _ _ Captain America.

d Captain America is m _ a n _ _ _ _ _ _ Lenda.

e Tino's brother, Alex, is y _ u _ g _ _ _ _ _ _ Tino.

f Alex is b _ g _ _ _ _ _ _ _ his little sister, Talita.

g Nakano has a l _ n g _ _ throw-in _ _ _ _ Tino.

h Captain America is c _ az _ _ _ _ _ _ _ everybody!

GRAMMAR

GRAMMAR CHECK

Prepositions of movement

Prepositions of movement tell us where something moves to.

Tino went past the defender.   *The ball went into the goal*

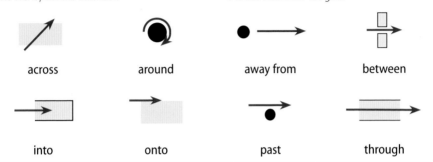

across   around   away from   between

into   onto   past   through

13 Complete the advice about football with the prepositions in the box.

  a Only go ..... *onto* ..... the pitch when the ref says 'OK'.

  b Run .... the box when there's a cross.

  c Shoot .... the posts!

  d As a forward, don't make a run .... two defenders.

  e As a defender, pass the ball .... the pitch to other defenders.

  f You can dribble .... one player, but perhaps not two!

14 Look at the picture. Complete the sentences about the player's goal with prepositions of movement.

  a He runs .... *across* .... the pitch and shouts for the ball.

  b He dribbles .... one midfielder.

  c He goes .... a defender.

  d He kicks the ball .... another defender's legs.

  e He blasts the ball .... the net.

  f He runs .... the goal to the fans.

  g The players put him .... their shoulders.

DOMINOES Your Choice

Read *Dominoes* for pleasure, or to develop language skills. It's your choice.

Each *Domino* reader includes:
- a good story to enjoy
- integrated activities to develop reading skills and increase vocabulary
- task-based projects – perfect for CEFR portfolios
- contextualized grammar activities

Each *Domino* pack contains a reader, and an excitingly dramatized audio recording of the story

If you liked this *Domino*, read these:

From the Earth to the Moon
Jules Verne

It is 1865. Impey Barbicane and J.T. Maston are very good with guns and explosives, and want to do something important – so they decide to build a big gun and use it to go to the Moon. But no-one has gone to the Moon before, and many people, like the great Captain Nicholl, believe that it cannot be done.
What will happen when Barbicane and Nicholl meet? And will the men who try to go to the Moon come back alive?

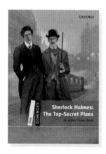

Sherlock Holmes: The Top-Secret Plans
Sir Arthur Conan Doyle

'This telegram is from my brother Mycroft,' said Holmes. 'He wants to speak to me at once about Mr Arthur Cadogan. Do you know this man, Watson?'
'I saw something about him in today's newspaper,' I answered.
When a young man dies on a London Underground line, top-secret plans for a new British submarine go missing. But who is Cadogan's killer, why did he die, and where are the missing papers? Sherlock Holmes and Doctor Watson must quickly help Mycroft to answer these important questions.

	CEFR	Cambridge Exams	IELTS	TOEFL iBT	TOEIC
Level 3	B1	PET	4.0	57-86	550
Level 2	A2–B1	KET-PET	3.0-4.0	–	390
Level 1	A1–A2	YLE Flyers/KET	3.0	–	225
Starter & Quick Starter	A1	YLE Movers	1.0–2.0	–	–

You can find details and a full list of books and teachers' resources on our website:
www.oup.com/elt/gradedreaders